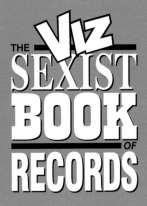

THE **Viz**
SEXIST
BOOK
OF
RECORDS

B▇XTREE

Editors' Foreword

If you had walked into the Rising Sun pub, Wallsend, on a cold October evening in 1955 you would have seen two brothers having a friendly discussion in a corner. They were arguing over the most times a man had ever had to ask his wife to iron his shirt. One said it was 706 times, the other maintained it was 710.

Eventually, one of the men broke his glass on the table and twisted it into his brother's face, who retaliated with a vicious headbutt. There seemed no way to resolve the dispute, so they agreed to differ and carried on drinking.

You will not be surprised to learn that **we** were those fighting men, and as we staggered to Rake Lane Hospital A&E at closing time we began to wonder: *What if there was a book which tabulated the world's sexist records, so that arguments of this sort could be resolved without the need for glassing?* The next afternoon, we sat down and began compiling just such a book. And so, the *Viz Sexist Book of Records* was born.

However, by their very nature, records are made to be broken and we found ourselves producing new, revised editions each year. And now we can hardly believe that this is the 47th edition of our book, with total worldwide sales exceeding 8 trillion.

During the near half century of its existence, the *Viz Sexist Book of Records* has taken its place on cisterns the length and breadth of the land, yellowing next to such illustrious volumes as *101 More Uses of a Dead Cat*, *The Purple Ronnie Omnibus* and Bruce Forsyth's autobiography.

Ross & Cromarty McBurger (Editors)
Newcastle, 2002.

And just for the record: Between the dates of March 29th and April 2nd 1953, Dennis Twelves of Hornchurch (GB) was forced to ask his wife Mary to iron his best shirt an incredible 986 times before she actually got round to doing the job. So we were both wrong.

First published 2002 by Boxtree
an imprint of Pan Macmillan Ltd
Pan Macmillan, 20 New Wharf Road, London N1 9RR
Basingstoke and Oxford
Associated companies throughout the world
www.panmacmillan.com

ISBN 0 7522 1505 1

9 8 7 6 5 4 3

A CIP catalogue record for this book is available from
the British Library.

Printed by Proost, Belgium

Contents

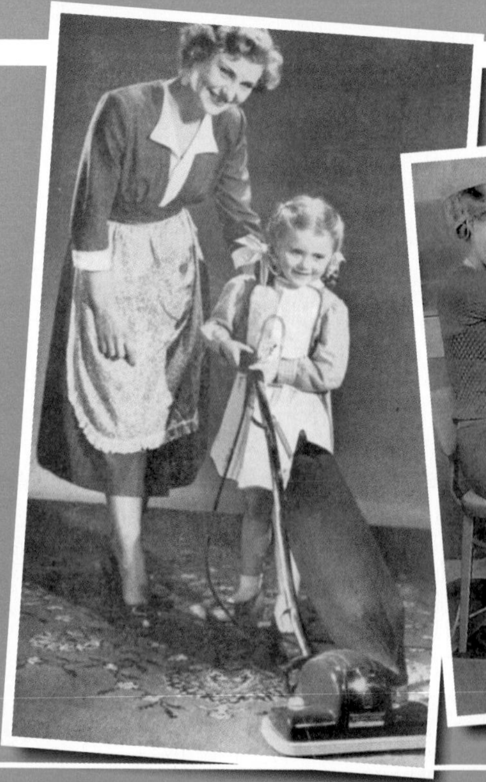
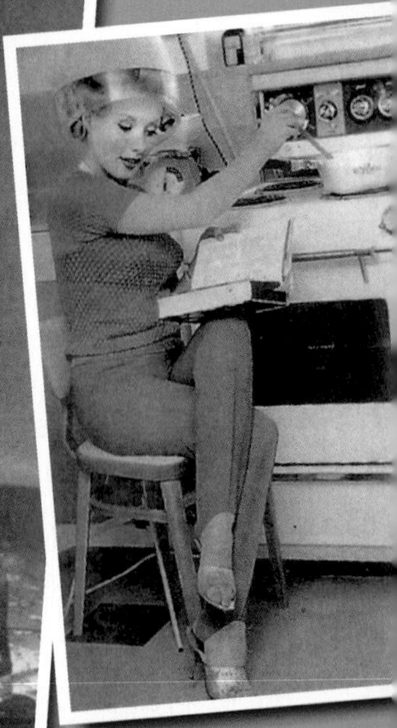

The World of Women

The World of Women

Driving

Car Parking

The smallest kerbside space successfully reversed into by a woman was one of 19.36m *63ft 2ins,* equivalent to three standard parking spaces by Mrs. Elizabeth Simpkins (GB) driving an unmodified Vauxhall Nova 'Swing' on the 12th October 1993. She started the manoeuvre at 11.15am in Ropergate, Pontefract and successfully parked within three feet of the pavement 8 hours 14 mins later. There was slight damage to the bumpers and wings of her own and the two adjoining cars, as well as a shop frontage and two lamp posts.

Most Lessons Without Pulling Away From Kerb

As of May 17th 2001, Mrs Eileen Tiptree (GB) had taken 2914 driving lessons without once feeling confident enough to pull away from the kerb or even start the engine. Her weekly lessons involve her getting nervously into the

Most Lessons Without Pulling Away From Kerb • Eileen Tiptree says goodbye to her 303rd driving instructor.

Incorrect Driving • Dr. Julie Thorn and the Saab 900 in which she made her record breaking drive on 2nd April 1987.

car outside her home in Chelmsford, Essex and sitting whilst her instructor once again patiently explains what the controls are. During one of her lessons in 1986, she plucked up enough courage to briefly waggle the gearstick to check the car was in neutral before fainting. She has so far spent over £50,000 on lessons, and been through 303 instructors.

Incorrect Driving

The longest journey completed with the handbrake on was one of 504 Km 313 miles from Stranraer to Holyhead by Dr. Julie Thorn (GB) at the wheel of a Saab 900 on the 2nd April 1987. Dr. Thorn smelled burning two miles into her journey at Aird but pressed on to Holyhead with smoke billowing from the rear wheels. This journey also holds the records for the longest completed with the choke fully out and the right indicator flashing.

Longest Roundabout Drive ·
The scene of the four-day marathon circumnavigation which ended in Dierdre Martin's death.

Longest Roundabout Drive

The late Miss Dierdre Martin of Canterbury (GB) holds the record for the longest continuous traffic island circumnavigation. Setting out for Sturry on Monday, March 2nd 1998, she entered a traffic island at the junction of the A2050 and the A28. Trapped by other vehicles, she found herself unable to take her chosen exit and decided to go round once more. 4 days, 3 hrs 16 min later, having rounded the island an amazing 5813.3 times, Miss Martin was still unable to reach her exit, and her Ford Fiesta ran out of petrol. A passing motorist stopped and topped her car up with a gallon *4.5l* of fuel, after which she continued for another 632 circuits before dying of natural causes.

Closest Seat to Steering Wheel

On 22nd August 1996, it was found that a Ford Fiesta 1.3 belonging to seventy-year-old Dierdre Martin (GB) had a seat to steering wheel distance of 14.6cm *6ins*. On short drives around her home town of Canterbury, Miss Martin reduced this to 11.1cm *4ins* with the use of a supplementary cushion, although she admitted that this led to some difficulty breathing.

Car repairs

The largest bill for fictitious work carried out on a woman's car by garage mechanics was one of £6322.88 charged by Joskin Bros Motors Ltd. of Stevenage, Herts. (GB). Calling in for a routine service on her one-year-old Peugeot 305, Mrs. June Spears agreed to pay for, amongst other things, new trumpets (£725), cracked gangle pin (£1785), realignment of main glib shaft (£2268), new grommets (£112), set of hexagonal tag nuts and dangleberry adapter (£35) and new piss-take valves (£120). No work was actually carried out on the car during the six weeks that it spent at the garage but 4000 miles were put on the clock and she later

Car repairs • June Spears, who was taken for a £6,322 ride by her local garage.

Right turning • The aftermath of Helen Tredwell's carefully considered manoeuvre.

received a speeding summons from Italian police.

Right turning

The record for the longest time spent waiting to make a right turn is held by Miss Helen Tredwell (GB) of Greater Manchester. At 2.30 pm on Saturday 16th June 2001, whilst driving to visit friends in Warrington, she approached a side turning on the A559 in Stockton Heath. Indicating right, she slowed down and stopped to wait for an adequate gap in the traffic to make her manoeuvre. After 3 days, 2 hrs 6 mins, she finally judged it safe to proceed and accordingly went to make the turn, only to find that her Vauxhall Cavalier was not in gear. She continued to wait, finally spotting a sufficiently large gap on the Wednesday evening after waiting 4 days 6 hrs 22 mins. She commenced the turn, in the process striking a motorcyclist and knocking him into the path of an oncoming lorry. During her mammoth extra-cautious manoeuvre, she called out the AA five times, twice to fill her car with petrol, twice to replace burnt out indicator bulbs and once to replace the clutch.

Most point turn

On 23rd March 1999, Maureen Templeton (GB) set out in her Daewoo Matiz to take her two children to their primary school in Bicester. After dropping them at the gates, she commenced a three point turn in the road. Her power steering-assisted 180 degree U-turn was eventually completed after a remarkable 1,723 separate forward and reverse manoeuvres. By the time Mrs. Templeton's car was facing the other way, the children had finished school, and it was time to take them home.

Traffic light cosmetics

The longest spell spent oblivious to traffic lights whilst applying make up was one of 1 hr 51 mins 38 secs by Ms. Janet Dodson (GB) at a road junction in the centre of Preston on the 1st August

Traffic light cosmetics • A section of the 28 mile grid lock caused by Janet Dodson in August 1975.

1975. Ms. Dodson, a piano teacher, beautified herself through 212 cycles of the lights, creating a tailback of irate motorists stretching 28 miles towards Leeds.

Blobstrops

Least provocation

Whilst menstruating on July 18th 2000, Susan Turpin of Leeds (GB) discovered her husband, James, had placed a spoon the wrong way round in the cutlery drawer after washing the dishes. Acc-

using him of being 'thoughtless and selfish' she burst into tears, attempted to stab him with a breadknife and moved in with her mother for a week.

Shortest fuse

The record for the quickest a woman has flown into a tammy huff was set on April 24th 1978 by Tina Wren of Arbroath (GB). Returning from an 18 hour nightshift as a security guard, her husband Alan began to ask if she would like a cup of tea.

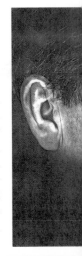

One fiftieth of a second (0.02 sec) after opening his mouth, he was hit full in the face with a frying pan.

Shortest fuse • Alan Wren after asking Tina if she wanted a cuppa.

Shop Dithering

The longest time spent dithering in a shop was 12 days between 21st August and 2nd September 1995 by Mrs. Sandra Wilks (GB) in the Birmingham branch of Dorothy Perkins. Entering the shop on a Saturday morning, Mrs. Wilks could not choose between two near identical dresses which were both in the sale. After one hour, her husband, sitting on a chair by the changing (continued on page 24)

British Girl Smashes Rag Rage Record

ANTIQUE dealer, Robin Smith-Chivers was yesterday counting the cost of unwisely jiggling his car keys in his pocket whilst his wife had the painters in.

Sarah Smith-Chivers was stock-taking with her husband at their exclusive Bond Street showroom when she took exception to the noise he was making and began throwing things at him.

During the following ten minutes, Mrs. Smith-Chivers managed to destroy artworks and antiques worth an estimated £8.5 million.

onslaught

Her husband, who suffered a cracked rib and bruised fingers in the onslaught was last night trying to come to terms with the loss of the business he has been building

- *a Regency mantle clock in marble, circa 1805 (£80,000)*
- *a 12th C Tung dynasty vase (£50,000)*
- *a painting of Charles I by Van Dyck (£1m)*
- *a Chippendale mahogany dining table and 12 chairs (£1.2m)*
- *3 Stradivarius violins, a 13th c Samurai suit of armour and a harp-sichord (£3m)*

A still hormonal Mrs. Smith-Chivers was last night unrepentant. "It's nothing to do with my periods," she told reporters. "It's those keys. He's always jiggling those f***ing keys in his pocket. I've told him a thousand times not to. Last night I just snapped," she added, before bursting into tears.

Smith-Chivers - unrepentant yesterday

up for the past 15 years.

Some of the items smashed and damaged in the attack include:

- *an 18th C silver coffee pot (£20,000)*
- *a 240 piece Sevres porcelain tea service, circa 1860 (£75,000)*

THE SEXIST TIMES

room with his head in his hands, told her to buy both. Mrs. Wilks eventually bought the one for £12.99, only to return the next day and exchange it for the other one. To date, she has yet to wear it. Mrs. Wilks also holds the record for window shopping longevity, when, starting on September 12th 1995, she stood motionless gazing at a pair of shoes in Clinkard's window in Kidderminster for 3 weeks 2 days before eventually going home.

Jumble sale massacre

The greatest number of old ladies to perish whilst fighting at a jumble sale is 98, at a Methodist Church Hall in Castleford, West Yorkshire (GB) on February 12th 1991. When the doors opened at 10.00am, the initial scramble to get in cost 16 lives, a further 25 being killed in a crush at the first table. A seven-way skirmish then broke out over a pinafore dress costing 10p which escalated into a full scale melee resulting in another 18 lives being lost. A pitched

Jumble sale massacre • The Rev. Julian Spriggs helps one of the few dazed survivors of his jumble sale.

Going out • Maria Cartwright, fourteen hours in, and nearly ready.

battle over a headscarf then ensued and quickly spread throughout the hall, claiming 39 old women. The jumble sale raised £5.28 for local boy scouts.

Social

Going out

At 6.08 pm on Saturday 14th January 1988, Mrs Maria Cartwright (GB) went upstairs to get ready to go out for a meal with her husband Nigel at their home in Pitlochry, Perthshire. She finally pronounced herself ready and came downstairs at 8.34 pm the following Thursday, 5 days, 2 hrs 26 mins later. During her marathon preparations, Mrs Cartwright had tried on and rejected 14,783 different combinations of clothing, jewellery, make-up and shoes. Her husband spent the entire time standing at the bottom of the stairs in his suit, jingling his car keys. He later estimated he had shouted up to ask if she was ready at least 750 times, to which he had received the response "Yes, nearly" on every occasion.

Talking about Nothing

Mrs. Mary Caterham (GB) and Mrs. Marjorie Steele (GB) sat in a kitchen in Blackburn, Lancs. and talked about nothing whatsoever for four and a half months from 1st May to the 17th August 1978, pausing only for coffee, cakes & toilet visits. Throughout the whole time, no information was exchanged and neither woman gained any new knowledge whatsoever.

The outdoor record for talking about nothing is held by Mrs. Vera Etherington (GB) and her neighbour Mrs. Dolly Booth (GB) of Ipswich, who between 11th November 1983 and 12th January 1984 chundered on over their fence in an unenlightening dialogue lasting 62 days until Mrs. Booth remembered she'd left the bath running.

Greatest Number of "she saids"

The greatest rate of "she said's in a woman's conversation was achieved *(continued on page 30)*

FASTEST FOOD!
-Hairdresser snips minutes off record

A PRESTATYN hairdresser has **SMASHED** the record for the shortest wait for a 'Fillet-O-Fish' at a McDonalds Drive-Thru.

36-year-old Beverly Charlton placed her order at the Denbigh branch of the fast food outlet and sat in the Red Grill Order parking space for just 1 hour 43 minutes before her meal arrived.

stories

She told us: "I couldn't believe it. I'd heard stories about people who got their Fillets-O-Fishes in under two hours, but I just thought they were urban myths."

delight

Beverly's delight soon turned to disappointment however, when on returning home she discovered that they had forgotten her fries. And given her the wrong drink.

29

during the recounting of a report of a report of a rumour of a conversation overheard in a launderette about a local woman's daughter possibly becoming pregnant. On September 14th 1998, Irene Scholes of Widnes (GB) managed to include the phrase "she said" 1283 times in 1 min 27 sec, an average of 14.7 "she said"s per second. During one 8 second burst of the conversation, Mrs. Scholes sustained an incredible peak rate of 38.3 she saids/sec

Gossiping • Mrs. Agnes Banbury of Cheadle. Britain's champion scandalmongerer.

Gossiping

On February 18th 1992, Joyce Blatherwick, a close friend of Mrs. Agnes Banbury (GB) popped round for a cup of tea and a chat, during the course of which she told Mrs. Banbury, in the strictest confidence, that she was having an affair with the butcher. After Mrs. Blatherwick left at 2.10 pm, Mrs. Banbury immediately began to tell everyone, swearing them all to secrecy. By 2.30pm, she had told 128 people of the news. By 2.50 pm it had risen to 372 and by 4.00 that afternoon, 2774 knew of the affair, including the local Amateur Dramatic Society, several knitting circles, a coachload of American tourists which she flagged down and the butcher's wife. When a tired Mrs. Banbury went to bed at 11.55 that night, Mrs. Blatherwick's affair was common knowledge to a staggering 75,338 people, enough to fill Wembley Stadium.

Single Breath S
Record Smashe

AN OXFORDSHIRE woman today became the first ever to break the thirty minute barrier for talking without drawing breath.

Mrs Mavis Sommers, 48, of Cowley smashed the previous record of 23 minutes when she excitedly reported an argument she'd had in the butchers to her neighbour. She ranted on for a staggering 32 minutes 12 seconds without

Motormouth Mavis breaks elusive half hour barrier

pausing for air before going blue and collapsing in a heap on the ground. She was taken to the Radcliffe Infirmary in a wheelbarrow but was released later after check-ups.

ntence

At the peak of her mammoth motormouth marathon, she acheived an unbelievable 680 words per minute, repeating the main points of the story an amazing 114 times whilst her neighbour, Mrs Dolly Knowles nodded and tutted.

croak

The last third of the sentence was delivered in a barely audible croak, the last two minutes being mouthed only, accompanied by vigorous gesticulations and indignant spasms.

THE SEXIST TIMES

Huff longevity

The longest recorded huff taken by a woman was one of 57 years 9 months 8 days by Mrs Glenda Bavington (GB). Following a misunderstanding over a sausage roll and an egg sandwich at a New Years Eve party in 1936, she went into a huff with her sister Betty and didn't talk to her again until their father's funeral on 8th October 1994. Despite working alongside each other on the bakery counter of the local Co-op in Aberystwyth, Dyfed for the first forty years of the record, Mrs. Bavington looked straight through her sister and pretended she wasn't there. At a New Years Eve party in 1994, the subject of the sausage roll was brought up again and the huff recommenced, lasting until Betty's death earlier this year.

Huff longevity
Glenda Bavington

Cinema

Video Lesbianism

The longest period of time that two women in a pornographic film have sat together on a settee without starting to fondle each other is 8.3 secs in the 1994 low-budget production of 'Strap-on Sally, vol 3' (US). The longest a woman has sat alone on a settee without fondling herself is 5.2 secs in the same film.

Film Confusion

The greatest length of time a woman has watched a film without asking a stupid plot-related question was achieved on the 28th October 1990, when Mrs. Ethel Brunswick (GB) sat down with her husband to watch 'The Ipcress File'. She watched in silence for a breath-taking 2 mins 40 secs before asking "Is he a goody or a baddie, then, him in the glasses?", revealing a staggering level of ignorance. This broke her own previous record set in 1962 when she sat through 2 mins 38 secs of '633 Squadron' before asking "Is this a war film, is it?"

Miscellaneous

Daytime TV

The greatest amount of Australian soaps watched in a single eight hour day without getting out of the chair was 34 hrs 28 mins by Mrs. Rita Cunliff (GB). This record was achieved using five television sets and three video recorders on 22nd January 1996. When Mrs Cunliff's husband returned from work he had to make his own tea.

Fluffy toys

The biggest collection of ridiculous fluffy toys on a woman's bed is one of 7046 belonging to 28 year-old Sharon Merson (GB) of Bodmin, Cornwall. The collection, weighing 857kg *1185lb* includes 2295 teddy bears, 1146 puppies and kittens, 1208 Garfields, 947 Paddingtons, 877 Snoopies and 573 assorted pigs, elephants and gonks - all with their own names! After kissing them all goodnight, a process which takes up to 5 hours, Miss Merson sleeps on the floor.

Fluffy toys • Sharon Merson of Cornwall ready for bed with some of her 7,046 fluffy friends.

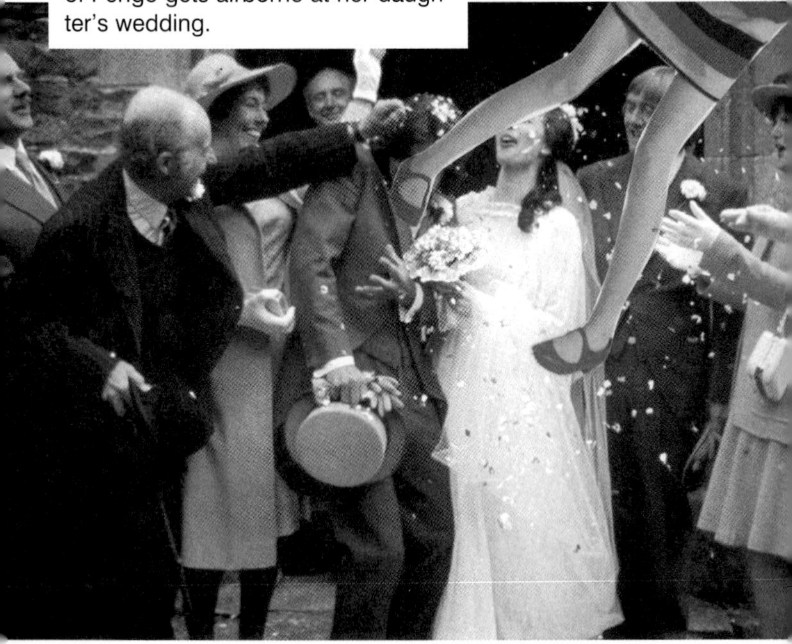

Wedding hat • Mrs Ethyl Acetate of Penge gets airborne at her daughter's wedding.

Wedding hat

The most extravagant piece of headwear worn by a mother of the bride at a wedding was a hat measuring 3.85m *13ft* high and 14.96m *50ft 5ins* across. The hat, which cost the lives of 110 assorted ostriches, peacocks and birds of paradise was constructed for Mrs Ethyl Acetate of Penge (GB) to wear at the wedding of her daughter Chantilly in 1997. Unfortunately, during the photographs on the steps of Penge registry office, a sudden gust of wind caught under the brim of the hat and lifted Mrs Acetate 40 feet into the air. She landed in a B&Q car park 100 yards away, suffering cuts, bruises and a broken ankle.

Ball throwing

The furthest distance a standard 155g *5oz* cricket ball was thrown by a woman was 2.28m *7ft 6ins,* slightly greater than the length of a standard house door, by Tricia Oldman (SA). The throw was made whilst playing for the South African National Ladies' Cricket Team against New

Zealand in June 1988, and was rewarded with a standing ovation from the crowd.

Group Toilet Visit

The record for the largest group of women to visit a toilet simultaneously is held by 147 workers from the Department of Social Security, Longbenton (GB). At their annual Christmas celebration at a nightclub in Newcastle upon Tyne on October 12th 1994, Mrs Beryl Crabtree got up to go to the toilet and was immediately followed by 146 other

Holiday romance • Tracey Spencer after her diarrhoea but before her moped crash.

members of the party. Moving as a mass, the group entered the toilet at 9.52pm and, after waiting for everyone to finish, emerged 2 hrs 37 mins later.

Holiday romance

The fewest number of sexual partners had by a woman on an 18-30 holiday is 17, by Miss Tracey Spencer (GB) between August 7th and 14th 1998 on a one week package to San Antonio, Ibiza. Miss Spencer attributed her chaste performance to the fact that she was hospi-

Flatpack furniture • Julie Medford of Ipswich shows off her rickety Klit.

talised with Crytosporidial diarrhoea for the first 4 days of the holiday and spent the last two days in intensive care following a moped crash.

Orangest skin

On March 4th 1995, Miss Kelly Marie Prestwick (GB), a sales assistant in the perfume department of the John Lewis store in Leeds was independently assessed by chromatologists from the Laboratoire Garnier as having a skin orangeness equivalent to 165 on the Pantone classification scale. This is about twice as orange as the skin of a satsuma.

Flatpack furniture

The most complicated piece of flatpack furniture more or less sucessfully assembled by a woman was an Ikea-bought Klit occasional table, put together by Julie Medford of Ipswich (GB). The piece, consisting of four screw-in legs and a flat top, took Miss Medford slightly over three weeks to assemble and was completed with only two pieces left over.

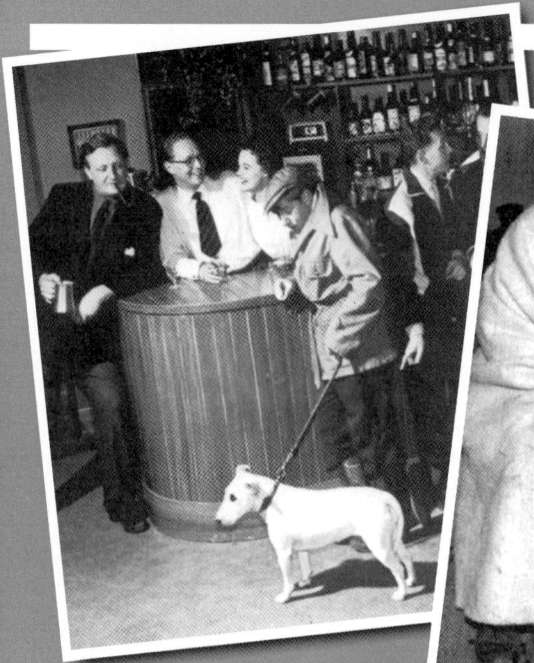
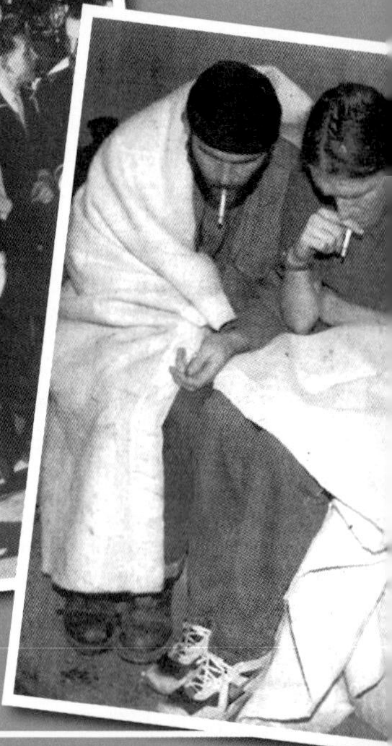

The World of Men

Most expensive drinks • A-level student Stephen Arundel steps out for an expensive night on the town.

46

The World of Men

Food and drink

Beer drinking

The greatest amount of beer drunk before going to the lavatory was 25.5 litres *45 pints* of assorted weak lagers by Mr. George Wingfield (GB), downed in various pubs in Knutsford High Street, Cheshire, between 12.15pm and 2.38pm on 22nd December 1986.

Most expensive drinks

The world's most expensive drink was sold from a van parked near the Spanish Steps in Rome (I). On the 8th August 1985, confused tourist Simon Dawes (GB) paid 12.5 million lire (£5000) for a standard 330ml can of Coca Cola. By way of comparison, the usual price charged in Rome for a can of soft drink is only 87,500 lire (£35).

The most expensive drink in Britain was a pint glass containing approximately 1/3 pint of beer and 2/3 pint of froth. Celebrating the end of his A-levels on 7th June 1996,

6th former Stephen Arundel of Keswick (GB) paid £315 for the watered down bitter at the Knockers-a-GoGo Club, a basement striptease establishment in Soho, London.

Most expensive bag of peanuts

On 7th June 1996, 6th former Stephen Arundel of Keswick (GB) paid £890 for a 70gm *2 oz* bag of salted peanuts at Jug-O-Rama, a basement striptease establishment in Soho, London.

Hottest curry eaten

Many claims are made about the ferocity of curries eaten, but in the main they are difficult to substantiate. The hottest verifyable curry eaten was a XXXHot Chicken Murg Thaal with extra chilies consumed by George Wingfield (GB) at the Bengal Tiger Restaurant, Knutsford on 23rd December 1986. The curry was reportedly so hot that between kitchen and table it burst into flames, singeing the waiter's eyebrows.

Most expensive bag of peanuts • Stephen Arundel's nuts cost him another £890.

Worst piles • The 5th Earl of Beaminster suffering nobly with his Chalfonts in 1902.

Physiology

Urinating

The longest piss delivered at one continuous scoot was one of 36 mins 24 secs by Mr George Wingfield (GB) in the doorway of a newsagents shop in Knutsford High Street on 22nd December 1986. Mr Wingfield was arrested and charged with a public order offence 17 minutes into his record attempt, but arresting officers had to wait a further 19 mins 24 secs before taking him back to the station for a kicking.

Worst piles

The worst piles ever recorded belonged to Sir Ernest Worthing-Bart, The 5th Earl of Beaminster (GB) (1865-1919). His ordeal began when he was speared up the anus at the Battle of Abu Klea (Egypt) in 1885. His haemorrhoids developed to such an extent that he was invalided out of the household cavalry in 1887. His condition worsened over the following years until by the turn of the century his anal blood vessels had reputedly swelled to the size of a bunch of tangerines. By 1905, Sir Ernest was a virtual invalid, spending weeks on end confined to a tractor tyre on his estate in East Sussex. He died tragically on a European tour after he became separated from his nurse, took a wrong turning and inadvertently became caught up in the Pamplona Bull Run, at which point he dropped his keys with disastrous consequences. Spanish doctors reported that at the time of his death, Sir Ernest had a

bunch of 38 haemor-rhoids, each of which was the size of a prize-winning pumpkin, accounting for over 95% of his body weight.

Biggest fart

The largest and most cat-astrophic fart was one dropped by Mr George Wingfield (GB) in the car park of the Dog and Duck, Knutsford on the morning of 24th Decem-ber 1986. Suffering from terrible guts, Mr Wing-field gingerly attempted to squeak one out whilst

Biggest fart • George Wing-field, holder of many of the least enviable records in this book.

Longest toilet visit • Les Schofield of Leicester, who spent three days reading on the chod bin.

54

bending to pick up his car keys, but the resultant flatulent explosion blew his entire digestive tract out of his arse. Attending firemen hosed down his smoking guts for two hours before paramedics with breathing apparatus could begin the process of pushing them back up.

Longest Toilet Visit

The record for the longest toilet visit (single defecation) is 72 hours, 18 minutes and 3 seconds, held by Les Schofield of Leicester (GB). Entering the bathroom at 11.14am on the 17th of July 1984, he sucessfully completed his bowel movement 34 seconds after sitting down. He remained seated, with his trousers around his ankles, reading an old copy of *Exchange & Mart,* eventually emerging shortly before lunch the following Wednesday. Mr Schofield did not regain feeling in his legs for 27 days, and the red elbow imprints on his knees were still visible to the naked eye 8 months later.

Testicular pressure

The greatest internal pressure sustained in a pair of testicles is one of 65 atmospheres *955lb/in²*, or approximately 49,400 mm of mercury at sea level, in the scrotum of the the pop singer Sir Cliff Richard (GB), following a 45-year build up of seminal fluid. This is equivalent to six times the pressure currently bearing down on the hull of RMS Titanic. It is estimated that were Mr Richard to ejaculate, the resulting jizzbolt would attain a peak altitude of 335m *1100ft*, comfortably clearing the TV mast on top of the Eiffel Tower.

Most evil fart

The most pungent flatulation ever was dropped by Balthazar Beauty of Babylon, a mature pedigree Newfoundland dog owned by Miss Eileen Dulwich (GB). The 63.4kg *140lb* animal had just eaten six tins of pilchards and eight tins of tripe mix, washed down with a gallon of milk when it dropped its guts on

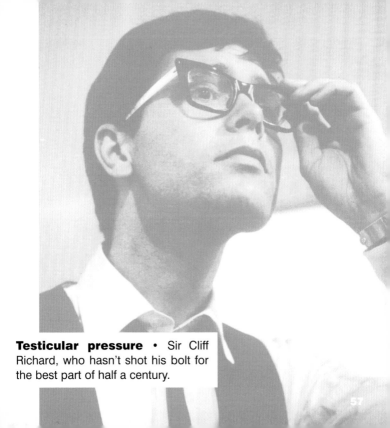

Testicular pressure • Sir Cliff Richard, who hasn't shot his bolt for the best part of half a century.

Most evil fart • Balthazar Beauty of Babylon, or 'Fartarse', as he is known to his proud owner, Eileen Dulwich.

BBC TV's *Record Breakers* programme. It is estimated that the resultant gaseous emission could comfortably permeate a building three times the volume of the Millennium Dome with a putrid aroma of rotting cabbage, Frenchman's breath and sewer gas.

Most viscous stool

The stickiest motion ever produced was a stool passed by driving instructor Eric Butcher of Leicester (GB). After being stuck in traffic for 5 hours in the hot summer of 1976 with nothing to eat but a 4lb box of dairy fudge and a bottle of cream soda, Mr Butcher went home to the toilet. The resultant excrement was so viscous that eight full rolls of standard Andrex toilet paper, approximately 1600 sheets, were needed before he attained an even vaguely acceptable level of anal cleanliness.

Pottest belly

The overhanging beergut belonging to Trevor Chisholme (GB) of Chorley, Lancs weighed in on July 7th 2002 at a mammoth 148.7kg *23st 6lb.* Not including his record breaking super pot, Mr. Chisholme himself would weigh a mere 49.3kg *7st 10lb.* He achieved this impressive feat in only 8 years of relentless heavy drinking, during which time his trouser waist size has remained the same whilst his pot has ballooned above his belt. Having a bilge tank the size of Mr. Chisholme's would be equivalent to walking around with World Champion shot putter Geoff Capes lying in the bottom of your vest.

Student early rising

On 12th March 1999, Tarquin Otterburn, a third-year philosophy student at Manchester University (GB), got out of bed in time to attend a lecture on Wittgenstein beginning at 11.30 am. He exited his bed at around 11.18 am in order to get to the lecture,

Student early rising • Tarquin Otterburn gets to grips with Wittgenstein in the wee small hours of the afternoon.

Uselessness • Rex Broadbent hard at work, doing all he was capable of doing.

with puffy eyes and his hair all stuck up. Doctors at the University Medical Centre gave him a check-up and pronounced him fit but exhausted after his feat, but warned other students not to try to copy his actions.

Holiday gymnastics

The greatest number of press-ups done in front of some girls on a beach is 6 by Wayne Fletcher (GB) whilst on holiday in San Antonio, Ibiza on 19th August 1988. The girls went off with a waiter.

Uselessness

The record for the greatest inability to do anything practical is held by Rex Broadbent (GB) of Preston, Lancs. During forty years of marriage, Mr. Broadbent's long suffering wife Freda, cooked, washed, ironed, did all the housework, held down two cleaning jobs and brought up six children while her husband, an unemployed gas fitter, watched the telly. On June 28th 1991, she went into hospital to have a hysterectomy, leaving Rex to fend for himself. However, unaware of where the kitchen was, he died of dehydration after just four days, waiting for his wife to come home and make a cup of tea.

Biggest Hockle

Whilst taking a lunchtime stroll from his local pub to the bookmakers on September 8th 1973, Patrick O'Dougle (GB) (1932-1974), a 180-a-day smoker (untipped) stopped momentarily on a street corner in Tipton, West Midlands, to eructate. The record breaking greb he produced was the size of a fully grown tabby cat and was described by horrified witnesses as looking a bit like black cauliflower cheese.

Miscellaneous

Most expensive box of matches

The most expensive box of matches ever sold in Britain was one costing £1350, an incredible £28 per match. The box was purchased on 7th June 1996 by 6th former Stephen Arun-

Biggest hockle • Patrick O'-Dougle, the man who brought up a two-gallon prairie oyster.

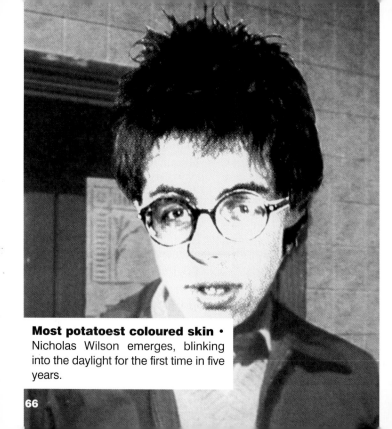

Most potatoest coloured skin •
Nicholas Wilson emerges, blinking
into the daylight for the first time in five
years.

del of Keswick (GB) in Tit City, a basement striptease establishment in Soho, London.

Most potatoest coloured skin

Nicholas Wilson of Largs, Lanarkshire (GB) holds the record as Britain's most translucent teenager. After devoting 5 years to reaching Level 30 of *'The Tomb Raider Chronicles'* in his bedroom with the curtains drawn, Wilson's skin was assessed to have a pasteyness value of 8.7 on the Maris-Piper scale, aproximately four times as pale as Shane McGowan.

Biggest student overdraft

Whilst studying economics at Aston University between October 1999 and May 2002, Miles Halsall (GB) ran up a student overdraft of £8.6 billion, equivalent to approximately twice the gross national product of Finland. He graduated with a third class degree, cirrhosis of the liver and terminal lung cancer. His wordly possessions consisted of two Terry

Pratchett novels and a furry pencil case.

Stiffest sock

A Marks and Spencer's wool/nylon mix Argyle sock found under the bed of Nicholas Wilson of Largs, Lanarkshire (GB) exhibited a tensile strength of 6.3 gigapascals $9.17x10^5lb/in^2$, and a Knoop hardness value of 8412. Scientists at Edinburgh University estimate that Wilson's sock, slightly harder than a diamond has been masturbated into more than 11,000 times since its last wash.

Train location notification

On February 12th 2001, Clive Head (GB), a deputy sales manager for UK Paperclips Ltd embarked on the 8 km $5.11 miles$ train journey from his workplace in Leeds to his home in Guiseley. During the 15 minute journey, Head used his mobile phone to call his wife Gaynor a staggering 138 times to report on his progress at the top of his voice. That's one call every 6.52 seconds, and at a to-

Stiffest sock • A scientist from the University of Edinburgh tests the hardness of Nicholas Wilson's sock.

Worst behaviour forgiven by a bunch of flowers • Serial bigamist William Soskin who 'said it with flowers' on June 29th 1989.

tal peak time cost of £34.50.

Worst behaviour forgiven by a bunch of flowers

On June 29th 1989, William Soskin of Wigan (GB) came home from the pub to find his enraged wife, Barbara, throwing his clothes into the street. Whilst going through his pockets she had found evidence that over the previous 30 years, Mr. Soskin had bigamously married at least four other women in the neighbourhood, fathering upwards of fourteen children by them. He had also conducted affairs with his wife's sisters and mother, by whom he had fathered a further sixteen children. He was completely forgiven after presenting his wife with a bunch of sorry-looking flowers costing £1.99 from the local all-night petrol station.

Rugby club good behaviour

The record for the longest a University Rugby Club has behaved in a seemly fashion is held by the

Rugby club good behaviour
• Keele University Second XV lose their battle against indecorousness.

Keele University Second XV (GB). During a charity fundraising attempt on 28th March 2002, the squad wore men's clothes, avoided setting fire to their farts, refrained from incoherent singing of indecorous songs, and kept their cocks out of each other's beer for 9 mins 14 secs before the prop forward put on stockings and shat into a pint pot.

Shelf putting up

The longest time that has elapsed between buying a shelf and putting it up is 113 years and counting, in the case of an ornament shelf leaning up against a wall in the home of Sidney Green of Cheltenham (GB). The shelf was purchased by his great grandfather Edward in October 1889, and despite constant nagging by their wives, four generations of Greens have so far failed to put it up. But there is good news for the present Mrs Green - Sidney intends to put it up next weekend, or the one after.

Expletives • Harold Brayson gets ready to turn the air blue.

Expletives

On 9th June 1996, Mr. Harold Brayson (GB) struck his thumb with a stone mason's mallet whilst breaking concrete in his back yard in Tewksbury, Gloucestershire. He went on to swear for 14 mins 7 secs without stopping or once repeating a swear word. He later attempted to better this feat on BBC TV's *Record Breakers* programme by dropping a car battery on his foot. It ended in failure when he repeated the word bastard after 12 mins 58 secs.

Starting

Scrapyard owner 'Fighting' Frankie Smith (GB) of Blyth, Northumberland, currently holds all UK starting records. In a 26 year starting career, he has started on no fewer than 35,577 innocent people, mainly in the pubs and clubs of Blyth and Ashington. On December 26th 1991, between 12.30 pm and 11.55 pm, he started on 512 people in the Dog and Hammer public house, the most ever achieved in a single day. Smith also holds the

Tit's a RECORD!

Leeds student smashes own annoyance record!

SECOND-YEAR Sociologist Giles Swift has broken his own record for **getting on people's tits** during a 4-hour session in Leeds city centre.

Talking loudly about his A-level results, paying for Rizla papers with his Barclaycard, and saying 'actually' at the end of every sentence, the 21-year-old wanker from Luton got on a total of 7928 people's tits.

He told reporters: "I've been practicing hard for the past 12 months, but it was still pretty difficult, actually. I could have done a lot better, only the supermarket was shut."

Next year, he hopes to pass the 10,000 mark on a busy shopping street with the aid of a mobile phone and a cumbersome rucksack.

A jubilant Swift after his record-breaking feat yesterday

THE SEXIST TIMES

record for the oiliest dog and most unstable pile of crashed cars.

Denying Christ

The record for the most number of times an apostle has denied the Messiah before the cock crows is thrice, set by Simon who is called Peter (Judea). His mammoth feat of foreswearance which has stood for nearly two millennia, was set in the early hours of Good Friday 32 AD, in and around the Garden of Gethsemane. Simon who is called Peter paced himself throughout the night, with his final denial coming just before the second crowing of the cock. When the record was confirmed by Pharisee Pethuel McWhirter from the Temple of Golgotha, Simon who is called Peter celebrated by going outside the city walls and weeping bitterly.

Hobbies

Most Screwdrivers Bought

Over a period of twelve and half years, Mr. William Bavistock of Mold, Clwyd (GB), is estimated to have bought more than 18,350 identical screwdrivers, all of which he knows are still somewhere in his house. Unable to find any of them, when Mr. Bavistock changes a plug fuse he invariably has to use a butter knife.

In 1968, Mr. Bolivio Gonzalez of Caracas (Venezuela), made an unsubstantiated claim that he had purchased over 26,750 flat-bladed screwdrivers, but the only one he could ever find was a Phillips.

Kiddly diddliest priest

The greatest number of altar boys interfered with by a single Roman Catholic priest is 83,254 by Father Finbarr O'Plywood (ROI). In a 62-year career in the church, O'Plywood has been the incumbent of over 1,100 parishes and has been the subject of 2,360 internal church investigations without any charges being levelled. He was recently promoted to Archbishop.

Kiddly diddliest priest • Father Finbarr O'Plywood, who has never been charged with any offence.

Longest time hiding on an allotment

Returning from a week's honeymoon on April 7th 1946, George Fairbrass went down to his allotment in Wakefield, West Yorkshire (GB) to hoe his sprout beds. He remained there, aimlessly pottering in his shed for 47 yrs 7 mths 25 days. He returned on 2nd December 1993, to find his wife, Dolly, had kept his tea warm for the best part of half a century. After eating, he went to repair some chicken wire in his pigeon loft. His wife has not seen him since.

Longest time hiding on an allotment • Mr Fairbrass outside the shed where he has spent the best part of his life.

Loudest car stereo

The Saisho stereo fitted in the Mk II Ford Escort belonging to Wayne Fletcher (GB) reached a momentary peak noise level of 312 dB whilst waiting at traffic lights next to some girls in Stockport, Cheshire on 8th July 1988. This noise level is equivalent to 8 Concordes taking off inside the car. The girls walked off.

Car Customisation

Judged as a proportion of

Car customisation • Wayne Fletcher, holder of a myriad of show-ing off records.

the overall value of the car, the accessories fitted to the Mk II Ford Escort of Wayne Fletcher (GB) add up to the world's most expensive car customisation project at 105,761%. Between 8th March 1986 and 22nd September 1996, Fletcher had spent a grand total of £63,456.99 at the Stockport branch of Halfords in an attempt to attract girls to his vehicle. His fruitless purchases include a Paddy Hopkirk Full Body Styling Kit (£3500), 'Nightrider' style Disco Stop Lights (£199), Split 45 Weber Carburettors x4 (£200), Scorpion Talking Alarm (£500) and a Chromium plated Mock Twin Exhaust Extension (£285). The car is currently valued at £50 to £60.

Longest wheel spin

The greatest length of time a car has screeched its wheels to impress some girls was achieved on 9th July 1988 by Wayne Fletcher (GB) in his Mk II Ford Escort. When traffic lights in Stockport, Cheshire turned green, Fletcher attempted to pull off at such speed that his front wheels spun for an amazing 42 secs before the car began to move. Both tyres fell to pieces and the clutch dropped off twenty yards down the road. The girls walked off.

Rep driving

The most impressive display of multi-task driving was achieved by Powdered Egg Salesman Mel Henshaw (GB) at the wheel of his Vauxhall Cavalier 2l GLi. On February 12th 1992, whilst driving at 112 mph in freezing fog on the M1 in South Yorkshire, he simultaneously shaved, ate a sandwich, dictated a letter, read a road map, filled in his expenses, re-tuned the radio, took his jacket off, smoked a cigarette and spoke to his wife on his mobile phone.

Pornography

Beating the clock

Whilst attending an ecumenical conference on 18th November 1998, Father Arthur Linehan of Letterkenny (Republic of

Rep driving • Mel Henshaw demonstrates his skills as he crosses the central reservation.

Ireland) switched on the TV in his room in the Travel Tavern, Liverpool. During the 10 minutes of free pornography before his screen went fuzzy, Fr. Linehan suceeded in masturbating to ejaculation 12 (twelve) times.

Strongest freestanding piece of furniture

In May 2001 it was reported that a wardrobe belonging to the writer and comedian David Baddiel (GB) was supporting a deadweight of over 210 tonnes *463,680lbs*, consisting of a portion of his collection of hardcore anal pornographic magazines. (At the time of going to press, it is believed that this mass has increased to approximately 304 tonnes *671,081lbs* after 200,000 borrowed copies of 'Skanda Clævøland Stæmør' magazine were returned by his friend Frank Skinner).

Hedgerow erotica

The greatest amount of torn-up pornography found under a single hedge was collected by 15 boys

from The Airedale Secondary Modern School in Yorkshire (GB). During a field trip to the Meikleour Hedge in Perthshire, Scotland (GB) on 1st October 1983, the excited youngsters harvested 2,032kg *4480lb* of shredded bongo mags. For the coach journey home, each child was carrying an estimated 135 kg *298lb* of porn up his jumper.

Hedgerow erotica • Pupils from Airedale school, who found over two tons of grummer in a single afternoon.

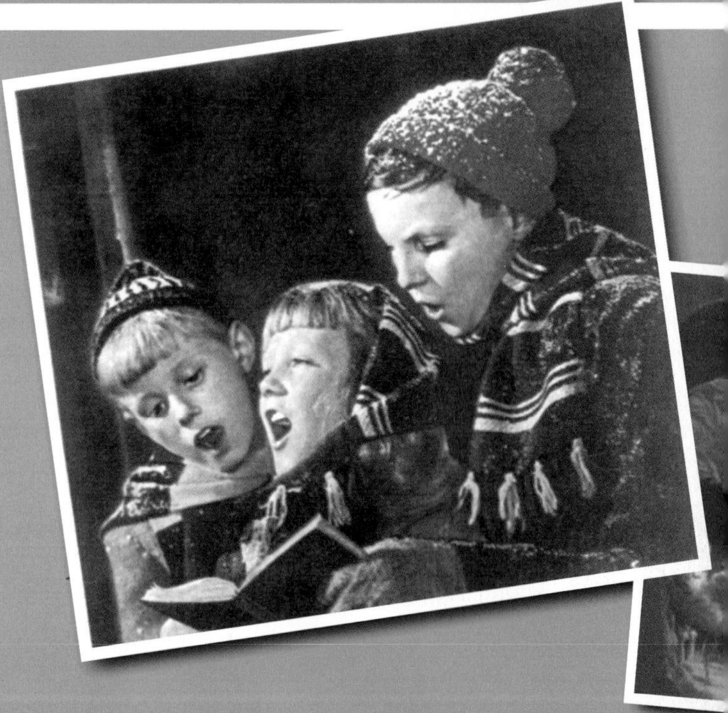

Christmas
Records

the First Christmas

Christmas Records

Date discrepancy

The record for the biggest disparity between dates eaten on Christmas Day versus the rest of the year is held by Phillip Runcorn (GB) of Derby. Between 8.30am and 11.30pm on 25th Dec 1998, he consumed a total of 23.456kg *51lb 12oz* of 'Eat Me' dates, despite not particularly liking them. During the previous 364 days he had eaten half a date weighing 7gm *0.247oz* whilst at his brother's wedding, an annual discrepancy of 23.449kg or 335214.28%.

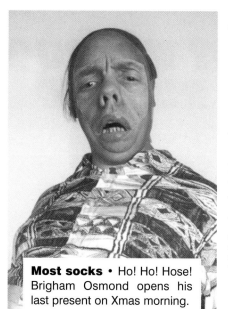

Most socks • Ho! Ho! Hose! Brigham Osmond opens his last present on Xmas morning.

Most socks

On Christmas Day 1996, Mr Brigham Osmond, a polygamous Mormon of Salt Lake City, Utah (US) received 847 pairs of socks from his ten wives, 84 children and 753 grandchildren. The following year, thanks to the addition of 2 more wives, six more children, 56 grandchildren and a great grandchild, he received 912 bottles of Pagan Man aftershave.

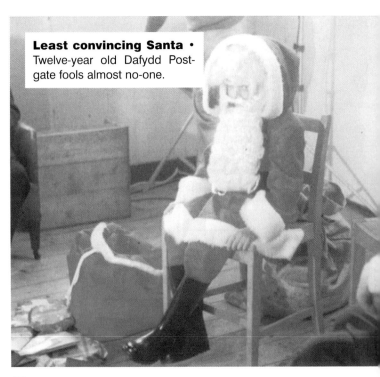

Least convincing Santa • Twelve-year old Dafydd Post-gate fools almost no-one.

Longest gift-related huff

On November 29th 1968, Margaret Pierce of Gateshead (GB), told her husband Ron not to get her anything that year for Christmas. When on Christmas morning she found that he hadn't, she embarked upon a huff which as of October 14th 2002 has lasted for 12,316 days. During this time man landed on the Moon, the Berlin wall has been torn down and a third world war has begun. Meanwhile, Mrs Pierce has sat with her arms folded, pretending to watch the telly and affecting not to hear her husband.

Least convincing Santa

In December 1998, in the Grotto at Claire's Department Store in Llandudno (GB), Dafydd Postgate managed to fool only three children, two of whom were blind, that he was the real Santa Claus. Postgate, the manager's 12-year-old son, was ordered to put on a cotton wool beard after all staff had refused. His high-pitched Ho! Ho! Ho's did little to convince the 687 children who visited the grotto that year, many of whom left in tears. Postgate estimated that he had had his beard pulled off over 500 times by irate toddlers.

Most Christmas trees behind shed

On January 6th 1946, Ernest Sands of Northampton (GB) put his Christmas tree behind the garden shed, intending to take it to the municipal tip that weekend. At the time of writing, Mr. Sands has 56 similar trees behind the shed, which he has had to extend five times to accommodate them. He intends to definitely take them to the tip this year.

Earliest wake-up

Henry and James Montgomery of Basildon (GB) were so excited about opening their presents from Santa on Christmas Day 1999, that they woke up at 2.33 am on October 25th 1998. Their bleary-eyed father Stephen told them to go back to bed, as there were still 14 months to go.

Arse photocopying

The record for the most photocopying of arses at an office Christmas party is held by the staff of Eversheds Solicitors in Newcastle upon Tyne (GB). On Dec 23rd 1987 a total of *6,938* A3 buttock copies were produced on a standard Sharp SF2035 copier. During the 4-hour party, 14 reams of paper were used, the toner cartridges were changed 8 times and the service engineer was called out twice.

Arse photocopying • The post-party remains of the Sharp SF2035 after Xeroxing nearly 14,000 solicitors' buttocks.

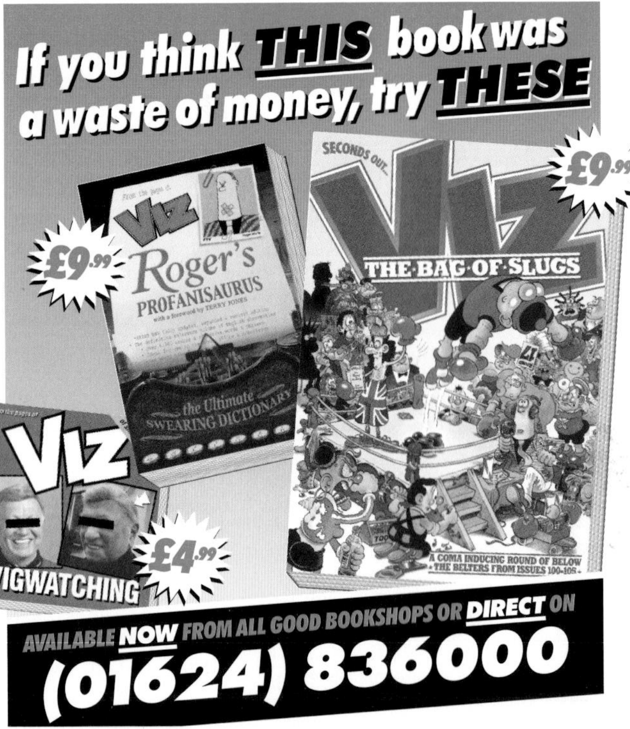
If you think THIS book was
a waste of money, try THESE
SECONDS OUT...
VIZ
THE·BAG·OF·SLUGS
A COMA INDUCING ROUND OF BELOW THE BELTERS FROM ISSUES 100-105
£9.99
VIZ
Roger's
PROFANISAURUS
the Ultimate SWEARING DICTIONARY
£9.99
VIZ
WIGWATCHING
£4.99
AVAILABLE NOW FROM ALL GOOD BOOKSHOPS OR DIRECT ON
(01624) 836000